SADIE and RATZ

Sonya Hartnett

illustrated by
Ann James

CANDLEWICK PRESS

For Hannah — who else?
S. H.

For Joan Haycraft
A. J.

Text copyright © 2008 by Sonya Hartnett
Illustrations copyright © 2008 by Ann James

First U.S. edition 2012

Library of Congress Cataloging-in-Publication Data is available.

Library of Congress Catalog Card Number pending

ISBN 978-0-7636-5315-6

12 13 14 15 16 17 LBM 10 9 8 7 6 5 4 3 2 1

Printed in Melrose Park, IL, U.S.A.

This book was typeset in Bembo Educational.
The illustrations were done in charcoal.

Candlewick Press
99 Dover Street
Somerville, Massachusetts 02144

visit us at www.candlewick.com

CONTENTS

Chapter One

I am Hannah. These are my hands. Their names are Sadie and Ratz.

We live in a house with my mom and dad and my stick insect, Pin. I want a dog, but Mom says I'm too young.

Until I am older, I can only have
a stick insect. "And Sadie and Ratz,
don't forget," says Dad. Sadie and Ratz
aren't animals. "But they behave like
wild beasts," says Dad.

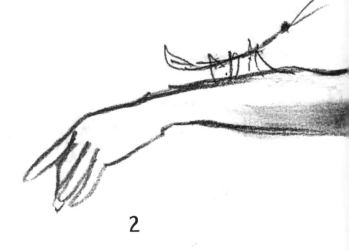

These are things I like:

purple
ladybirds
ponies
soft toys with sad eyes

When I am kind, these are things I do:

tickle Dad's ear
stroke Mom's hair
wobble Grandma's stomach

These are things that Sadie and Ratz like:

crunching
squishing
squeezing

They also like piranhas.

Sadie is the boss. She is the same size as Ratz, but she is meaner.

When Sadie grows up, she wants
to be a dragon. When Ratz grows up,
he wants to be a bigger Ratz.

Ratz does what Sadie tells him to do.
Together, they make a good team.

This is what they do:

crush things up
twist and scrunch
scratch! scratch!
scratch!

When Sadie and Ratz are on the
rampage, look out!

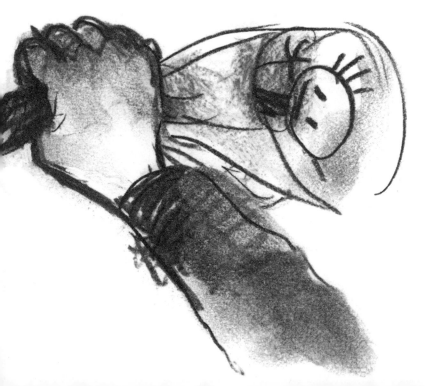

There is someone in our house
I forgot to mention.

Baby Boy

I wish he was a dog.

'Boy' by Hannah

Baby Boy is four years old. Four years is a long time. It seems like Baby Boy has been around forever.

Everyone says Baby Boy is a good boy. But these are things that Baby Boy does:

goes into my room

changes the TV channel

uses all the colored markers

When he does these things, Sadie and Ratz **wake up!**

13

They jump onto Baby Boy's head, and try to rub his ears off.

Baby Boy doesn't like it. He bellows like a banshee bull. Baby Boy bellows and then I get in trouble, even though Baby Boy caused the trouble in the first place. If he didn't annoy me, Sadie and Ratz wouldn't have to rub his ears off.

Mom says I must be patient. She says, "Baby Boy is only little." She says Sadie and Ratz should do yoga. She says, "They might learn to relax."

These are yoga positions Mom thinks
Sadie and Ratz could try:

"Snowflakes in Winter"

"Starfish"

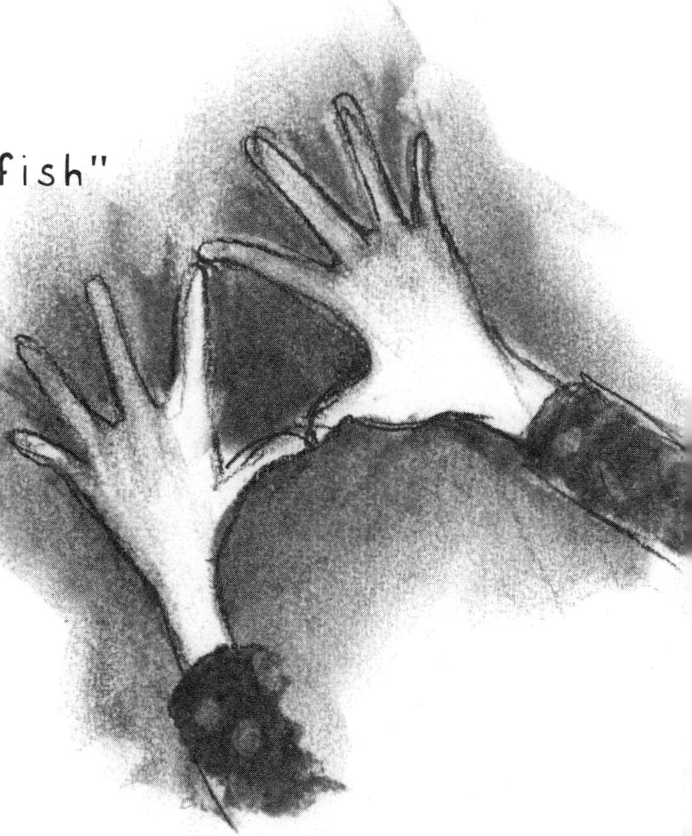

"The Rambling River"

Sadie and Ratz invented their own positions:

"The Lion's Mane"
"The Hammerheads"
"Long Lightning Bolts"

They showed Baby Boy the Hammerheads. He screeched like a banshee bull.

Chapter Two

On Saturday, at our house, something strange happened. I was drawing pictures, and Baby Boy was wandering around. Suddenly some marker was on the wall. It was a long black line on the clean white wall.

"Who did this?" asked Dad.

This is when the strange thing happened.

Normally Baby Boy would pretend
he hadn't heard Dad's question. He
would pretend he was a spaceman
who couldn't hear a sound. Instead
of owning up to drawing on the wall,
he would act like he was deaf.

But this day, this strange day, Baby
Boy yelled, "Sadie and Ratz did it!"

Sadie and Ratz **woke up!**
They showed Baby Boy their claws.

But Baby Boy was hiding behind
Dad, safe from attack.

"Sadie and Ratz should be more
careful," said Dad, scrubbing the wall.

Baby Boy peeked out at me, and
smiled like a crazy monkey.

Later, after dinner, when Baby
Boy was playing with trucks, Sadie
and Ratz showed him their new
yoga position:

"The Shark's Teeth"

Baby Boy did the banshee bull thing.
I got sent to bed.
As usual.

That was a strange day, but things were
about to get stranger.

On Sunday morning, when milk got
on the carpet, Baby Boy told Mom,
"Sadie and Ratz did it."

That afternoon, when he skinned his knee, Baby Boy told Grandma, "Sadie and Ratz pushed me."

Even though Sadie and Ratz had not spilled milk or pushed Baby Boy, I didn't say anything. I just gave Baby Boy a cold stare.

Grandma gave Baby Boy a kiss and a cookie. I only got a cookie.

I could not understand why my brother was telling these fibs. Maybe he wanted his ears rubbed so hard they disappeared.

That night, when Baby Boy was in bed, Sadie and Ratz and I crept into his room. "Do you want your ears rubbed off your head?" we asked.

Baby Boy's eyes made circles. He was about to yell like a whole herd of banshee bulls. Sadie and Ratz had no choice but to **attack!**

Mom and Dad came running. I got *The Stern Talk*. Baby Boy got more kisses.

Everything was wrong.

At school on Monday,
I took my lunch to
a corner where
nobody goes.
I needed
'some private
time. I ate my
sandwich and
thought.

Baby Boy was only four, but he was becoming tricky.

It was better when he was a spaceman who never heard or spoke. Sadie and Ratz liked doing bad things, but they didn't like getting in trouble for bad things they didn't do.

But everyone knew Sadie and Ratz were naughty. Everybody believed the worst when it came to Sadie and Ratz.

I ate my sandwich slowly. I wondered what Baby Boy was doing at home. I wondered what he was breaking or wrecking. I wondered what Sadie and Ratz would get the blame for today.

37

A horrible thought came into my head. Maybe Sadie and Ratz would have to change. Maybe the only way to stop Baby Boy blaming Sadie and Ratz for everything was to tame them, and make them nice.

No! I couldn't do it. It would break Sadie and Ratz's hearts.

39

Because they were sad, I let Sadie and Ratz have a war with each other. Sadie won, but it was close. They are both good fighters.

Chapter Three

On Tuesday, my stick insect, Pin, was missing a leg. At breakfast, he had six legs. At dinner, he had five!

This was too much.

I made the noise like the banshee bull.

"Baby Boy stole Pin's leg!" I wailed.

"Don't be silly," said Dad. "It probably just fell off. Maybe Pin ate it? Insects do funny things."

"Pin did not eat his leg!" I thundered. "Baby Boy pulled it off!"

"Baby Boy is a good boy," said Mom. "He wouldn't do something as naughty as that."

I jumped up and down. I kicked the wall. "If *he* didn't do it, who did?"

From where he was hiding, in the laundry basket, Baby Boy shouted, "Sadie and Ratz!"

But even Mom
and Dad knew that
Sadie and Ratz
wouldn't hurt Pin.
Mom looked at Dad.
Dad looked at Mom.
Both of them looked
worried.

I started to cry. "Baby Boy will get Pin out of his cage, and Pin will escape, and Dad will step on him!"

"No, no," said Mom, "I'm sure he wouldn't do that!"

"Oh no!" said Dad. "I'm sure I won't do that!"

But neither of them looked very sure about anything.

Something peculiar was going on in our house.

That night, Sadie and Ratz wanted to rub Baby Boy's ears, nose, hair and chin right off his head. But I knew that would cause more strife. Baby Boy knew it too. Baby Boy was little, but he was crafty.

I said, "Sadie and Ratz, you must go on vacation." It was the best idea I had. If Sadie and Ratz were far away, Baby Boy couldn't get them into trouble.

Sadie wanted to go where they make movies.

Ratz wanted to go where there were pinball machines.

They waved good-bye, and set off on vacation.

The next day, I was lonely. I was sad at school. At home, I lay on my bed and drew pictures, and ate some cheese sticks. I took Pin out of his cage and let him wobble up my arm.

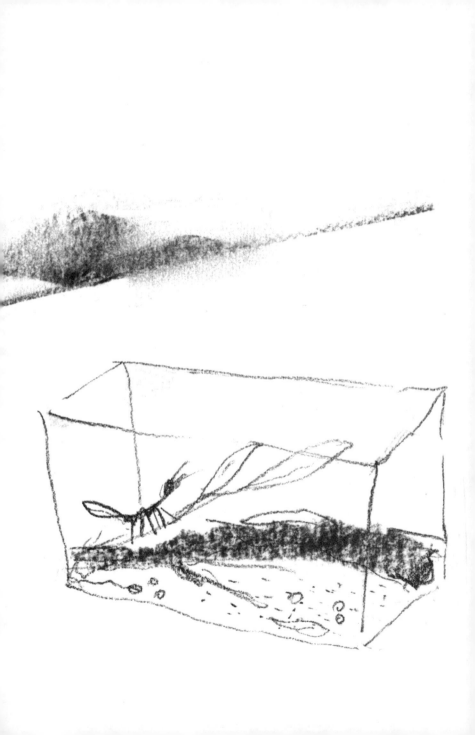

When Pin had had his exercise, I
put him back in his cage.

I sighed.

I missed Sadie and Ratz already.

Suddenly Baby Boy bellowed.
Mom, Dad and I followed the sound.
Baby Boy was standing in the sitting
room, pointing to Mom's
precious clock. It was
a tiny clock. It was a
hundred years old.
It lay on the floor
in a hundred pieces.
It wasn't making its
usual ticking noise.

Mom's eyes made circles. "What happened?" she asked.

"Sadie and Ratz," said Baby Boy.

"That's not true!" I shouted. "Sadie and Ratz are on vacation!"

"I didn't do it!" said Baby Boy.
Mom and Dad looked at me,
and then at Baby Boy. Mom picked
up some bits of clock. The
bits were tiny. The
biggest bit was
the clock's
round face.

The small hand was pointing to the number 2.

The big hand was pointing to the number 12.

Mom said, "The clock stopped ticking at two o'clock."

At two o'clock, Sadie and Ratz had been playing pinball, and I had been at school.

Dad wouldn't break Mom's clock, and Mom wouldn't either, and neither would Pin.

Which left only one suspect.

But Baby Boy was a good boy. At least, that's what everyone thought.

And then we guessed who had *really* been drawing on walls, spilling milk, stealing legs and breaking clocks.

We all looked down at Baby Boy's hands. Baby Boy smiled like a happy, crazy monkey.

"Oh dear," said Dad.

"Oh no," sighed Mom.

"Hooray!" I said. Because when Sadie and Ratz came home from vacation, they were going to meet two new friends.

Baby Boy said their names were

Colin and Scraps.